Puffin Books

Dear Emily

Maria is fourteen and lives in a high-rise flat in the inner suburbs. Emily is six months older and lives on a farm.

Maria sees herself as sophisticated and cynical and a 'very interesting person'. Emily talks about nothing but her horse, her boyfriend and her pink frilly bedroom.

Maria feels very superior to Emily and her country ways. But why does she spin such fantasies in her letters to Emily? Why does she avoid meeting her?

In this very funny book we learn about Maria's problems with her weirdo mother, her boring father and her horrible brother G. F. Smales. This is a very entertaining account of a most unlikely friendship.

Maureen Stewart

Dear Emily

Puffin Books

Puffin Books
Penguin Books Australia Ltd,
487 Maroondah Highway, P.O. Box 257
Ringwood, Victoria 3134, Australia
Penguin Books Ltd,
Harmondsworth, Middlesex, England
Penguin Books,
40 West 23rd Street, New York, N.Y. 10010, U.S.A.
Penguin Books Canada Limited,
2801 John Street, Markham, Ontario, Canada L3R 1B4
Penguin Books (N.Z.) Ltd,
182-190 Wairau Road, Auckland 10, New Zealand

First published by Penguin Books Australia, 1986
Copyright © Maureen Stewart, 1986

Typeset in Ballardvale by
Abb-typesetting Pty Ltd, Collingwood, Victoria
Made and printed in Australia by
Dominion Press-Hedges and Bell, Victoria

CIP

Stewart, Maureen, 1939–
    Dear Emily.

    ISBN 0 14 032059 8.

    I. Title.

A823'.3

Dear Emily,

You don't know me. I have chosen you to be my penfriend. Our English teacher said it would be a good thing if we all chose a penfriend, as it would help with our writing. I chose you from a list of people wanting penfriends in last Sunday's paper. I hope you haven't had so many letters that you can't reply to me.

I chose you for two reasons. I like the sound of your name, and you live in the country. I've only been to the country once (so I'm told, I was only one at the time).

I'll tell you a bit about myself. I am an intensely interesting person. I've worked hard at being interesting, because I'm not much to look at. I blame that on my father, who is one of the least impressive human beings you would ever see. My name — would you believe — is Maria. I hate it. There are five Marias in our class. I am by far the most exciting of the five.

I live in Richmond, in Melbourne, with my glamorous mother and scruffy father, and a brother who is best ignored. I go to South Richmond High, and I'm fourteen, just.

My mother is an executive with a cosmetics company (actually she sells Avon stuff door to door, but what I said sounds more impressive, if you know what I mean). My father is a public servant and does nothing.

I could tell you more about myself and my family but it has just occurred to me that would be a waste of time, as you mightn't answer this letter.

I bet you are the only one called Emily in your class. Please answer soon and tell me about yourself and your family and everything.

Your penfriend (I hope!)

Maria Smales

Dear Emily,

Thank you for your letter! I am so glad you will be my penfriend. I will answer your questions first.

1. No, I don't have braces on my teeth. Mind you, I probably should have, as they are a bit much — I mean, too much of them, and they stick out a bit when I smile, but with my lifestyle I don't get to smile much so I suppose it doesn't matter all that much.

2. My hair is brown and my eyes are blue.

3. Yes, I get pimples, and there is a simple reason for this. For some time now my mother has been a vegetarian and a health food freak and so I don't get to eat normal things like chips and pies and soft drinks, so my skin suffers terribly, and so does my stomach.

4. I don't share your love of magazines! I think they are trashy. The ones my mother reads are all about clothes and makeup and diets and I was bored by them by the time I was ten. She might be glamorous but her mind is pretty slight.

5. No, it is not a contradiction to say that my father is in the public service and does nothing. I suppose you don't have public servants in the country, so you wouldn't know about them. Actually he is a clerk in the railways but I prefer to

call him a public servant. It makes him sound more intelligent then he really is.

6. I can't answer questions about my brother, because he is really best ignored, as I mentioned in my first letter.

7. No, I suppose I didn't sound intensely interesting in my letter, but you see, Emily, I didn't know if you would reply, and so I didn't tell you much about myself in case I was wasting time.

But now that I know I'm not, here is more information about me. I hate all herb teas and I detest mushrooms, eggplant, zucchini, and anything made from soya beans. Soya beans taste like mud. Most food my mother cooks contain some of the above detested foods. Are there any vegetarians in the country? I suppose not, because you eat cows and sheep and things there. Do you have any cows or sheep? You said your father was a farmer. That must be wonderful. Does he wear jeans and a cowboy hat? My father wears grey suits and it matches his grey job and grey personality. He sort of melts into the footpath.

I think I began to be interesting when I was about four. That's when I saw through fairy tales and bible stories.

8. No, I don't know what I want to be when I finish school. I might write television scripts, or work in a pet shop. Why do you want to be a cabi-

net maker? Why don't you try for some job outside in the fresh air, like maybe the person who holds the flag for roadworkers? I've thought of that one myself.

I'd better close now, because I've got some maths homework. You are so lucky to have a cat and two dogs. We live in a flat and can't have animals. It must be wonderful to live in the country. What do you have for breakfast?

Your penfriend,

Maria

P.S. No, I didn't get any Valentine cards. I think they are silly and fit for tiny minds like my mother's. She got three.

Dear Emily,

I didn't mean you had a tiny mind!

You mustn't take things so personally. And I wasn't rude about the magazines you like. I just don't like them myself. Did I really say they were trashy? I forget, but, if I did, I'm sorry. I mean, they are of course, but I shouldn't have said so. Some people get so easily hurt. I am not one of those people, I can take anything.

I can't believe you haven't heard of soya beans or eggplant. You are so *lucky*! And I'd give anything to have bacon and eggs most mornings for breakfast. We have home made muesli and I won't tell you what it looks like. It tastes like it too.

What I meant by my father melting into the footpath was not that he gets fainting attacks. I don't know if you have ever been to Melbourne, but the footpaths are grey, and so in his grey clothes he sort of looks like part of the footpath. Do you have footpaths in the country?

And, Emily, I wasn't trying to be smart about seeing through fairy stories and bible stories. I *am* smart, I don't try to be. How was I supposed to know you were a Christian? Live and let live, I say, but you wouldn't. You'd say 'an eye for an eye and a tooth for a tooth', wouldn't you? I suppose your parents made you believe in the tooth fairy and

Santa Claus, too. At least even my dad didn't try any of that with me. You believe what you like, and I'll do likewise.

But what do you mean when you write that 'it's nice for children to believe in fairy stories'? *Nice?* To believe in talking wolves that eat grandmothers? And wicked stepmothers who try to poison their stepdaughters? I mean, did you *really* believe in Little Red Riding Hood and Snow White? Do people in the country all believe in things like that?

What are your dogs called? What's your school like?

Your friend,

Maria

Dear Emily,

Thanks for your letter, and the photos of your dogs. I like their names. I mean, calling the black one Blackie and the white one Snow shows a sort of imagination, don't you think?

Your school sounds terrific. All that grass, and trees! Our playground (it's called that, believe it or not, even though it's a high school) is all cement.

Thanks for your photo. You look really cute in your uniform. Are long skirts coming back into fashion? I'll get one of myself for you. Is that your mum with you in the photo, or your grandmother? She looks nice, anyway. Wait till you see a photo of my mum — she looks like a model. Unfortunately, I didn't inherit her looks, but fortunately I didn't inherit her brain either.

Emily, I didn't say that country people were stupid. How could I say that when you are the only one I know? And I never generalise. And I certainly didn't say you probably believed in the tooth fairy. I meant you probably did *years* ago, when your baby teeth were falling out. And so what if you did? You made some money out of it.

Here's the Avon catalogue you asked for. I wouldn't buy any if I were you. I suppose you don't have Avon ladies in the country because it's too far to walk between farms. Mum said to thank your mother for her pumpkin scone recipe. She is going to make some tomorrow, when she has her Assertiveness Group. Does your mum go to those too?

No, my father doesn't go to Rotary meetings. I asked him why not, and he said they were for small men who toasted the Queen. My father's tall, and he wouldn't hurt a fly, so I guess he wouldn't fit in at a Rotary meeting.

Your boyfriend sounds interesting. No, I don't have one at the moment. As I've mentioned, Emily, I don't look attractive or anything, and I don't think boys like interesting girls anyway. They like them pretty and dumb, and I'm neither of those!

Anyway, that's all for now. Since you asked, my brother's name is Gregory Francis Smales, and he's sixteen and, no, he hasn't a girlfriend. Who'd have him?

If you really want to get some Avon stuff, the violet cream perfume is okay.

Your friend,

Maria

Dear Emily,

I gave Mum your Avon order and she'll send the stuff up to you next month. She's very pleased to get a new customer. You'll like the lip gloss, it tastes like strawberries.

Emily, you really mustn't take things so seriously. Honestly, I didn't say you were dumb! I suppose I should keep a copy of my letters to you to check what I *did* say. And I didn't mean you weren't interesting. I was just generalising about the sort of girls *most* boys liked. It doesn't mean that *you* are like that. A generalisation is only a generalisation, don't take those things seriously!

Do *all* country people take things so seriously? I suppose life is more serious in the country, what with cows and sheep and droughts and floods and bushfires and things. We city people sort of learn to live with things.

I asked Mum to explain what her Assertiveness Group did, so you can tell your mum about it. She says it meets once a month, and teaches women to be more assertive.

I overheard bits of a meeting once, and I tell you, they were about the most assertive lot of people I've ever heard. No one listens to anyone else, they all rap on about how they've been 'cultured' (I think that was the word — maybe it was 'culti-

10

vated') into being polite and submissive because they were female. Talk about crazy — my dad's the polite and submissive one around here. And they made so much noise!

Tell your mum they loved her pumpkin scones. Submissive means that you give in to other people all the time (I looked it up).

Fancy having all those cows! Lucky you like milk. Who milks them? Do you have machines for that? I've seen them on telly. How often do you have to milk cows, anyway? Do you have special names for them all? Yes, of course I liked your dogs' names. What made you think I didn't?

There's a parent-teacher night at my school next week. Do they have those in the country? I suppose not, because the towns are so small parents would know the teachers anyway. They probably talk about you in the supermarket.

I played some April Fools' jokes at school today. Do you have April Fools' Day in the country? One kid in our class pretended to have an epileptic fit which wasn't really very funny. I thought it was a bit sick, but at least it stopped the maths lesson for a while while the ambulance came.

My dumb brother played a vile trick on me this morning. I bought a cream bun from the milk bar to take to school for lunch, and he took the cream off and replaced it with Dad's shaving cream. I nearly threw up. You wonder why I don't like him? He's an apology for a human being.

Mum gave me a recipe to send to your mum but I threw it away. It was for soya bean vegetarian loaf, and you'll all thank me, believe me. It tastes like bad mud and you'd hate it, and why should you eat awful stuff like that when you live with cows and can have steak and milk every day.

My dad's got a promotion, which means he gets more money for doing nothing. I think he moves papers from his desk to other desks, at least that's what he says he does. You are lucky your father has a real job with animals even if he does toast the Queen.

I am pleased you are enjoying your talks with your boyfriend, Emily. Is he going to be a farmer, or does he have ambition?

I'll let you know how parent-teacher night goes.

Your friend,

Maria

P.S. No, I don't say my prayers at night. Who'd listen?

Dear Emily,

I suppose you are right, playing April Fools' jokes is a bit childish. Especially putting shaving cream on buns.

Emily, I didn't mean that farmers don't have ambition. You are a very sensitive person, I can tell from your letters. You ought to pray that you won't always be so sensitive. I wish my dad was a farmer, didn't I tell you that? Mind you, he's got no ambition whatsoever. He said yesterday he 'just lives from day to day'. Don't we all?

It is very kind of you to suggest that God would listen to my prayers. I tried it out. He didn't. I prayed that my brother would not stay in the bathroom for twenty minutes in the morning and that I'd top the class in maths. No go. In fact G. F. Smales was in the bathroom for twenty three and a half minutes this morning and I just scraped through maths. I guess, if there is a God, he doesn't have all that much power really. I mean, look at all those Africans starving. If you think about it, Emily, you'll see what I mean.

Parent-teacher night was a washout. The only teacher who has any time for me at all is my English teacher, and that's only because I like English and read books. Your teachers sound great. I suppose that's because country kids are really quiet and like a lot of animals really and don't cause discipline problems. It's a jungle in the city (or so my father says).

Your school bush dance sounded great fun. Your dress sounds lovely, I can see you in it, especially with a darling name like Emily. I'd look awful in pink frills, just horrendous. But then most people would. I guess they wear that sort of thing in the country, and why not? I am happy for you about your boyfriend. You seem pretty keen on him, I must say.

Our school is having a disco next Saturday night, but I don't think I'll go. A bit too childish for me, I'd rather stay home with a book, wouldn't you?

G. F. Smales found that photo you sent me (the one of you and your mum, not the dogs) and said he thought you were a spunk. That's the sort of horrendous comment he makes. I'm sure he is a terrible disappointment to my parents.

The Avon stuff *is* coming, they just take time, that's all. Does your boyfriend like make-up? I suppose he does if he likes pink frilly dresses.

I can hear my mother being *very* assertive to my father in the kitchen (it's his turn to cook tonight and he bought three steaks and a vegetable pie for mum but she hates meat in the house and she's screaming something about dead cows in her kitchen). Now, Emily, don't get sensitive about that. I know you have dead cows in your kitchen, or rather, pieces of them. I only wish we did more often. One more vegetable quiche and I'll throw up.

Do your parents ever fight? I suppose not, they're probably all idyllic and gentle like country creeks.

I'd better go. I tell you, it's a jungle down here.

Your friend forever,
Maria

Dear Emily,

You really don't know what a quiche is? And nor does your mum? You are certainly a very lucky person.

Thank you for your two letters. And I love the photo of you and Kevin at the bush dance. Your dress does suit the occasion, so does Kevin.

No, I didn't go to the disco. I said I wouldn't. Not my scene, really. G. F. Smales did, and I'll let you in on a secret. He took some rum and coke in a coke bottle and got *plastered*. He's going to turn into one of those dreadful male creatures who think it's clever to get *plastered*. I've heard my mother talk about them. I bet no one does that in the country. It's so childish, isn't it?

Mum says she's glad the Avon stuff finally arrived. She said don't bank on it working with Kevin, because it doesn't work with my dad, but you didn't order any men's cosmetics, did you?

My mother has changed her diet again, for the *worse*. She will only eat uncooked things. So we have to take turns at cooking what we want, while she nibbles carrots and celery and fruit and nuts. She gets these crazes every few months. I can remember years ago she ate bananas and milk for weeks, and that was all. As I have told you, Emily, she has a very small mind.

Thanks about your advice on God. I've tried again, with no result. If God's up there, he sure isn't tuned in to me. I can't believe all your family go to church! We never go anywhere together, not even for a picnic. I can't imagine my mum and dad singing away in a little building somewhere and looking all pure, and as for G. F. Smales, he'd get drunk on the communion wine or whatever you drink there at half time. I know about that because I went to a church when I was young and everyone lined up to get a drink. I will try again, Emily, I promise, because it can't do any harm to ask for good things to happen, and who knows? One day I might be lucky!

Look up 'idyllic' in the dictionary. Maybe country creeks aren't like that, but poets often use that word about country places. I hate to say it, but I'm glad your parents fight too. I guess they all do, like kids really. I mean, I can't stand G. F. Smales, so why should parents like one another? They aren't even related really, they just get together and make other people related.

I like getting your letters, they make me think, and there's not much thinking done around this flat, I can tell you.

You asked what the flat was like. It is *grandiose* (look that up). Flats in the city are wonderful, they have huge rooms and central heating and air conditioning for summer and everyone gets to share a swimming pool on the top storey.

What's your farm house like?

Your friend forever,

Maria

Dear Emily,

Thank you for your letter and the bookmark with GOD LIVES on it. I bet he's not too keen on living in Ethiopia right now, I wouldn't be.

And thanks for the photo of your house. It looks lovely! I thought you lived in a farm house, but it looks more like a mansion. I don't understand when you say it's falling down around your ears and it leaks. It looks grandiose. I haven't a photo of our flat right now but I'll send one when I have.

Swimming pools on top storeys don't crash through the other flats, Emily, because city engineers know how to build these things.

I am glad you explained the significance of the wine at church. I'm very ignorant about the religions of the world, although I have read about Hindus not eating cows, which seems a pity really because so many of them are so poor and I've seen pictures of cows roaming in the streets of India. Still, as I always say, live and let live.

Your bedroom sounds idyllic. Frilly bedspread and matching curtains. I should have known they'd be pink! My bedspread (I call it a doona, that's the name we use in the city) is like the Australian flag, and I have blinds, not curtains.

In the city we have blinds so people can't stare

in. It wouldn't matter in the country, because who cares what cows see?

No, I don't like any pop groups. You see, Emily, they date so quickly! You just get to like one, then another one comes along, and it takes so much time to keep up with them. I liked Abba when I was very young and my mother said it just showed I had no musical taste at all, like my father. He has no ear for music whatsoever. To him there are only two songs — one is 'Advance Australia Fair' and the other isn't.

Here's a new Avon catalogue. The pink Princess soap shaped like a heart should suit you just fine.

Your friend forever,
Maria

Dear Emily,

Hey, I just love that pretty pink writing paper you got for your birthday! You should have told me it was your birthday. Mine's 18th January. That means you're about six months older than me, but I guess no one would ever be able to tell that from your letters.

I hope you like your present which you'll get with this letter. Seeing you're so into photos I thought this would match your room, and you can put one of you and Kevin in it. I know I haven't sent you any photos yet, but I will. My father's camera is broken but he says he'll get it fixed.

Fancy getting a cassette player from your mum and dad! That's a terrific present. I got one when I was ten and really loved it at that age. As the ads say, I hope you get 'many hours of listening pleasure' from it. I did.

I didn't mean you had cows outside your bedroom window watching you, Emily. How was I to know they're kept in paddocks far away from the house? Yes, we do live rather high up — our flat is on the tenth floor. But that doesn't mean people can't look in. I mean, in the city helicopters and planes go past all the time, and you never know who could be in them.

And, anyway, at night when the lights are on,

people from other flats can look in, and who'd want that?

Of course I'll send you a photo of my beautiful mother, just as soon as we get a camera.

School is a bit dull at the moment. Just lots of assignments about things that don't really interest me. I mean, Emily, do you care about bushrangers? Or the rivers of Australia? Oh, I suppose you do, being in the country and all, but it hasn't got much to do with my life at the moment.

G. F. Smales is being very difficult. He wants to leave school and go on the dole and go surfing up north. My father says it is a waste of the taxpayer's money to do that, but G. F. Smales says where do Dad's taxes go anyway, and they might as well go to him. My mother is now into meditation so she doesn't say much, not that it would be worth listening to.

I am worried that I have the only working brain in my family. Tell me, are your parents clever?

Lots of love,
from your penfriend forever,
Maria

Dear Emily,

I know I've just written, but maybe you can help me. We have to do a project on bushrangers. Do you have any in the country? What are they like? I guess they don't ride horses now — maybe motor bikes?

Anyway, I would like to read your thoughts on this subject.

Till I hear from you,

Love,
Maria

Dear Emily,

Have just been reading more about bushrangers and I realise they were centuries ago.

I'm sorry to have troubled you for information which doesn't exist. If I'd read more about the topic I'd have known that, and I'm such a quick reader I'm amazed I didn't.

Maybe bank robbers are today's bushrangers. I'll take that line, anyway. You couldn't help with that because banks are in the city.

Does your mother meditate?

Love,

Maria

Dear Emily,

So glad you liked the photo stand. Yes, I thought you'd like the pink lace, and the heart shape. Mum says thanks for the Avon order. I just *knew* you'd order that soap!

Yes, I was a bit stupid about the bushrangers, I admit. I think people should always admit it when they are stupid, don't you?

To meditate means you just sit there and think of nothing, a bit like my dad does at work, though I can't see it's done him much good. My mum wears special clothes to meditate in. There must be a fortune out there for someone who makes these special clothes, like those things she wears for aerobics or whatever she calls it.

Talk about dumb! Mum just sits there on her bedroom floor all cross-legged and probably cross-eyed too but she closes her eyes so you can't tell. I asked her what she meditated about and she said, 'Nothing, Maria, that's the point of it. You just empty your mind.' It wouldn't take her long to do that.

Did I say we didn't have a camera, and also say we had a broken one? I suppose it's the pressure of city life, it makes you confused. Yes, we have one, and Dad is getting it fixed.

I didn't mean you were too old to get a cassette player. My mother has one. It's just that *I'm* too old for that sort of thing. You must read my letters really carefully to pick up that sort of casual mistake. I'm glad you find them so readable.

I don't agree with you that planes and helicopters don't fly low enough to see in my bedroom window. When I was about seven a police helicopter flew right past my window, and the pilot looked in, and so did his passenger. Who knows what I might have been doing? And yes, we do have other high flats right near us. You probably don't have Housing Commission Flats in the country, just Housing Commission farms.

It is nice that you think your parents are clever. How come they are farmers, then? I was reading in the paper that farmers don't make much money and that it's a hard life even when there's no drought.

I'm glad your dad agrees with mine about G. F. Smales' idea of the dole and surfing. I am constantly amazed my parents produced an interesting person like me. G. F. Smales is just what you'd expect them to produce. Maybe I'm adopted?

I asked my father that, and he said, 'Unfortunately, no,' whatever that means. *Then* my mother said, 'Adopted kids are wanted.' I ask you, Emily, where does that leave me?

No, I haven't tried praying again. I will soon. It is so good to know I have a true friend like you.

Love forever,

Maria

6th August,

Dear Emily,

You would not believe what has happened here. I keep your letters in my *private* drawer, and G. F. Smales has read some of them! I caught him in the act, so he didn't read them all. What a nerve!

He wants to *write to you.* I told him that would be a complete waste of time, because:
1. You have Kevin and don't need a boyfriend
2. You are my friend, not his
3. You are a simple, idyllic country girl who does not need to read about his useless urban pinball parlour lifestyle
4. You might catch a social disease from touching his notepaper.

All this has probably had some effect, so maybe you won't get a letter from him. After all, you don't reply to mine very quickly, so how could you write to *two* people?

If you do get a letter with dirty, messy writing on the envelope, burn it quickly before you all come down with a disease.

Yours, in warning,

Maria

Dear Emily,

It is very nice to hear that your mum is worried about me but for the life of me I can't think why.

What do you mean you didn't know I lived in a Housing Commission flat and they don't have heating and air conditioning or swimming pools on top? They *do*. You just haven't seen one, that's all, Emily, and I bet your parents have never been to a city either.

As for your dad saying that people would queue up for years to get a Housing Commission flat if they had huge rooms and pools and heating, well, tell him they *do*. They can be on waiting lists for years. We were, and we had to live with my mum's sister and her husband and three screaming brats while we waited, so, I tell you, people really want these flats. You ought to come down here some-time and have a look at our place. Your house might be a country mansion, but our flat is gran-diose and a city marvel. People go up and down in the lifts all day, it's a hive of activity. G. F. Smales used to go up and down in lifts for hours after school because he met such unusual people.

But then, the city's like that. A hive of industry, so I've read.

Of course some farmers are clever. You do take

things the wrong way still, Emily, although we are old friends now. I guess it takes country people a long time to catch on to some things.

And I didn't generalise from that one helicopter when I was seven! Who said that? Your dad, I'll bet. *You* would never grab onto something like that, you are so kind.

How nice that you put your photo taken with Kevin at the local show in my photo holder. Thanks for the photo of you on your horse at the show. Did you all ride horses there, or did your mum and dad go by car? We don't need a car in the city because trams go past all the time.

My mum says trams are like men, because if you miss one, there'll be another one along in a minute. I'm not sure what she means, but she seemed pleased when she said it, and as she doesn't say much, I'll pass it on for what it's worth. Probably nothing.

Our local show is a *huge* affair, have you heard of it? The Melbourne Show. We get a day off school. I used to go when I was small and such things impressed me.

That's all for now.

Love forever,

Maria

Dear Emily,

Lucky I got your letter and can reply so soon, otherwise you'd have called and found no one home.

Fancy you all coming down for the Show! And you come every year and show your horses and cows! I can't believe it! Is it because some city people haven't seen cows and horses before? I suppose it's all very educational for them.

Unfortunately we are going away for a week. Dad gets holidays and we're off to the Barrier Reef to cruise around and look at the coral. Otherwise I'd have loved to have you all come for lunch or whatever.

Maybe next year?

Lots of love, must pack for my holiday,

Maria

Dear Emily,

Yes, I'm sorry we missed one another too. Couldn't be helped.

I am so glad you enjoyed the show and one of your cows got a ribbon. What for? What will it do with it?

The reason you didn't see any pools on top of the Housing Commission Flats at Flemington is because you have to get right on top to see it. And yes, I agree those flats look pretty bleak outside, but that's to discourage burglars. I mean, if we made our flat look good outside, we'd be robbed! So the idea is to make it look as ordinary as possible to discourage people from breaking in. You get pretty hard living in the city, Emily.

I think it was very unfair of your parents to stay at the Regent Hotel and leave you out with the horses, but then I suppose you are used to that. How can you mean you prefer it at the Show with the horses to staying in a posh hotel? You are probably just excusing their behaviour (your parents' behaviour, not your horses').

Our holiday was wonderful. You must go there sometime. There's lots of coral and water.

Promise photos are coming of our holiday, as well as all the others.

I didn't know you'd been to Melbourne every year for the Show. Here I was thinking you were a simple country girl, and you're nearly as well travelled as me!

Lots of love,

Mania

Dear Emily,

Fancy you having been to the Barrier Reef too! Wow, for a country person you have certainly been around. They say (or so I've read) that travel broadens the mind. Well, not always, I guess. From your letters you haven't changed at all since I've known you.

Well, about your photos. Dad says he won't get the camera fixed, because we are all unphotogenic (look it up). At the moment I don't have a camera (I had one when I was eight but lost it at Ayers Rock) but when I get one again I'll certainly send some photos. *Promise.*

I am so sorry about Blackie dying, but, as you say, he was getting old. You should have prayed to God to save his life. Yes, I have tried praying again. I prayed that Dad would get his camera fixed, but, as usual, God wasn't tuned in to me. Maybe I'll pray that I'll get a camera for Christmas.

No, our school doesn't have end of year barbecues. They are probably worried some of the nastier kids would set fire to the school and not the barbecue. Things get pretty tough here in the city. But of course, I forgot, you know that, because you've been here every year. But I suppose if you're sleeping with horses you wouldn't get to see all that much.

All we have are end of year fights when kids squirt shaving cream around the place.

Glad you got your Avon stuff. Treasure it, because my mum's given that job up. She says that in order to make cosmetics, people experiment with animals, and she has joined Animal Liberation. She has even given up wearing make-up, so, when you get those photos, she'll look very different. Amazing what war paint can do! She looks really ordinary now.

At least she's eating cooked food again, which is easier for us, I can tell you. But a potato and zucchini casserole isn't exactly my idea of heaven, and that's what she made last night. I bet you have roast dinners and cake and things at night.

Hey, Emily, I got an A for my bushranger project! I thought Mr Watson had forgotten about it but he suddenly brought them back yesterday. Most times teachers at our school set work and sort of forget about it. I think it's because of the discipline problems.

Mum said to ask if your chooks are free range.

Lots of love,

Maria

Dear Emily,

Thank you for your letter and the bookmark GOD CARES. I hope he's caring about the Ethiopians right now. I know I do, and I'm sure you do. I'm even eating mushrooms and zucchini rissoles to prove it, because they would give anything for even that crummy food.

I told Mum your chooks are free range and she said you must be a lovely caring family. I said yes, you probably are, but you had so much room it would be easy to have free range chooks.

It's a bit like saying rich people who give money away and never steal are really great people. They probably are, but if you aren't poor, you don't have to think about stealing, do you? But Mum, as I have often mentioned, doesn't think too deeply. I reckon rich people can *afford* to have good morals.

How much pocket money do you get?

I do wish you would stop asking questions about G. F. Smales. He is so vile he even buys cheap keys to hang on his belt so people will think he has a car. He is not simple and nice like Kevin, he's always trying to impress people. Thank goodness I don't need to do that!

Why don't you have Blackie stuffed? I was reading the other day how a lady from a rich suburb had her dead budgie stuffed and it's in a cage and she can look at it any time she wants. Of course I realise Blackie would be buried by now but with the drought and all he'd be pretty well preserved. They probably have animal stuffers in the country (they're called *taxidermists*) because there are so many animals and probably one dies every day.

Then you could always remember him.

I wish I had a dog.

Love forever,

Maria

Dear Emily,

I don't know why you got so upset at my suggestion about Blackie. I was trying to be helpful.

I've never had a dog, and I'd love one, and I was thinking about your dog. I wasn't being nasty at all.

Please forgive me. Christians forgive, you know, so get into it and do it. Pray to God, he'll help you.

I won't write again until I hear I am forgiven.

I hope God cares about *both of us* because I want our deep friendship to continue.

Yours faithfully,
until I am forgiven,
Maria Smales

Dear Emily,

I know I said I wouldn't write again until you forgave me, but it just struck me that it will be Christmas soon and I was wondering what you'd like for a present.

We have some bits and pieces of Avon stuff around still that Mum used for samples, so would you like some of them?

Or maybe some pink writing paper?

Or pink ribbons?

Please let me know, because I like to plan my Christmas shopping early.

Yours faithfully,

Maria

Dear Emily,

What about frilly pink socks? I saw some lovely ones at the market the other day, and thought how well they would go with all your pink things.

I also saw a *wonderful*, *idyllic* pink lace pillow that would look terrific on your bed.

Please think about it and let me know.

Your friend, always,
Maria

P.S. *Please* forgive me about Blackie! I've never had a dog, and I didn't know how upset you'd be, honest. I mean, if G. F. Smales died (that I should be so lucky!) I wouldn't want him stuffed, because I'd want to forget him!

P.P.S. I must seem very insensitive to you. I think that comes from living in a Housing Commission flat, where all sorts of things happen all the time. A sensitive person wouldn't last here, I tell you.

Dear Emily,

I was so pleased to get your letter. If you'd waited any longer to write I would probably have just given you up. I am glad that God helped you understand my insensitivity. Thank him from me, personally, next time you pray.

Yes, you're right, the pink lace pillow sounds too expensive. It is. What do you think of the socks idea?

Well, I'm not sure what I'd like. I thought of asking you to send postage stamps, because it gets expensive sending letters and I think we will write to one another for ever.

But it's probably not such a good idea, because they keep putting the price of stamps up, so those you sent me would sort of go out of date. I know, I'd like some classy notepaper, like you use, Emily. You must be sick and tired of reading my scrawl from the back of railways memo pads. It's just that we always forget to buy writing paper, and Dad brings home these memo pads all the time. He probably never uses them at work, because there's nothing to remind anyone of there.

Mum is really into the Animal Liberation thing. She won't buy things made of leather at the moment. When I think about it, it's better than some of her interests have been, and I guess she has a point. You wouldn't believe this, but she's taken to wearing *overalls*. A bit like those farmers wear in margarine ads on telly, but brighter. She looks terrible, especially from behind.

I think it's this Assertiveness Group that has changed her appearance. She says things like, 'It's not the way you look, it's the way you are that counts' which I've *always* known. I mean, she's just discovered this at thirty-six! The sad thing is, all she really had going for her was the way she looked, which, as I've told you, *was* terrifically beautiful.

Your skirt and blouse for the school barbecue sound lovely. Do you think it's wise to wear pink and white? I suppose you're not messy like me — I'd drop sauce all over myself. Not that I've ever been to a barbecue, but I've seen them in ads on telly. Are you looking forward to Christmas? I'm not. It's never much fun here, really. My grandparents all live in other states and anyway Mum doesn't like Dad's parents and he doesn't like hers so it's probably a good thing. Mum drinks too much at Christmas and so the chicken is always burned and we never get to eat until about three in the afternoon if then.

Tell me what you do at Christmas, Emily.

Your dear friend, forever,

Maria

Dear Emily,

Your Christmas sounds idyllic!

I've never had turkey. What's it like? No, Mum doesn't eat the burnt chicken at Christmas, she eats the vegetables and drinks lots of wine out of a cardboard cask.

You are so lucky to have so many relatives come. You must get heaps of presents. I sent your present yesterday, I hope you like it. I've bought Dad a six pack of toilet paper, because he's always complaining that we run out of it, and Mum says she shouldn't always be the one to buy everything all the time, so I reckoned he could keep his own rolls in his bedroom cupboard and then he'd stop carrying on about the shortage of toilet paper in the Smales household.

I thought of buying G. F. Smales some rat poison, but the spirit of Christmas got the better of me, and I've bought him an underarm deodorant, which he needs, believe you me! I bought Mum a book, *How To Stop Feeling Guilty About Housework*. She doesn't do much of it, but she feels guilty about not doing it, so I thought it might help her. It's written pretty simply, so she shouldn't find it too hard to get through.

Yes, the pool is lively this time of year. After school we all laze around in it for hours, and there's even a waiter service for cold drinks. Your dam sounds great for swimming, and I suppose it's better than nothing if you haven't got a pool.

No, we're not going away for the holidays. The Barrier Reef was our holiday for the year! I just spend the time lazing around the pool and reading and seeing how many days I can spend not speaking to G. F. Smales, who is still talking about going north and getting the dole, which would be the best Christmas present I could get, I tell you!

Does your mother get drunk at Christmas?

Your friend forever,

Maria

Dear Emily,

I received your present today. Emily, you really shouldn't have! I've never held a camera before, let alone owned one. You are a true friend.

I'm glad you liked your socks and bookmark. I really couldn't think of anything else, and I'm sure, since so many relatives are coming to your place for Christmas, that you'll get loads of nice things. I don't know what the words on the bookmark mean either. Mum got it from her Women Against War group so it must be anti something or other. They all are.

I have one, too. She said, 'It will make you think, Maria. Send one to Emily, too.' So there you go. All it makes me think about is where I'm up to in my book. I ask her why she joins all these groups now, and she says she's 'raising her consciousness'. Honest, Emily, sometimes I despair of adults.

Of course women are against war. I am, aren't you? Why join a group and tell everyone about it? They're all against it too or they wouldn't join. I give up.

Thanks for the film too. I'll take some pictures, promise. Only two days to go to the dreaded Christmas Day. The chicken's frozen and we have frozen peas and packet gravy. At least the potatoes aren't frozen, though if Mum sees frozen roast potatoes, we've had it. Remember she was onto health foods? Well, that's all past. Now it's *time-saving* foods.

I'm glad your mother doesn't get drunk at Christmas. You are very lucky, Emily. Your mother sounds great. I think it's the pressure of city life that starts Mum off, really.

Thank you again for my camera. I will treasure it always.

Have a cosmic, unreal Christmas, and please write and tell me *all* about it. I love getting your letters.

These flats are pretty dull during the holidays. Your end of year barbie sounded idyllic. I think I'll live in the country when I leave school.

Yours, in Christmas spirit,

Maria

Dear Emily,

I just had to talk to someone, so, even though I only wrote to you two days ago, here I am again.

We have just finished Christmas dinner and it was just as I predicted. Burnt chicken and the frozen peas stuck to the pot. The potatoes were burnt too but I like burnt potatoes. Mum drank too much moselle and she and Dad had a rip roaring fight about the dishes. She said she cooked the meal so he should do them. I helped her cook, so I said G. F. Smales should help Dad do the dishes, but G.F. took off to the pinball parlour and that's the last we'll see of him today (forever I hope). So the dirty dishes are still on the table and Mum's watching telly and getting stuck into the moselle and Dad's gone to sleep.

What a Christmas!

You know, lots of my friends' parents have split up. I wish mine would. I often suggest it to them, in fact. I mean, anyone can see they are so badly matched. It was sort of okay when Mum tried to look pretty but now that she's into these strange groups and wears overalls, she really hasn't got much going for her.

And Dad is just a dull person. He can't help it, and I suppose I do love him really, but I think he'd be quite happy living with someone in the railways department and they could send one another memos all the time and never talk. I mean, he never talks to any of us.

I know I shouldn't be boring you with all this, Emily, but you seem such an understanding person. Soon I'm going to go in and wake Dad up and have a serious talk with him (Mum's beyond talking to) and see if he won't leave.

It must be so fascinating to come from a broken home! I'd give anything for that.

Till I hear from you,

Your friend forever,

Maria

P.S. Have you or your parents any advice on this problem of my parents? I think people must think more clearly in the country, with all that fresh air and no smog.

Dear, dear Emily,

Thank you so much for your letter, and the New Year's card. I'm sorry I didn't send you one. People don't send New Year's cards in the city, I suppose it's a country custom. It's a really nice idea.

Oh Emily, what a pity about the fire on Christmas Day! Here I was, feeling all sorry for myself because Mum and Dad were at one another's throats, and you were all fighting a bushfire! How lucky that your house wasn't burnt down. That's awful about the cows. I hope they died quickly. I suppose you couldn't eat them? A sort of unplanned barbecue?

Anyway I am very pleased for you that you were able to save what you could. Fires must be horrible things. Sometimes we have them in the city, but they are pretty easy to control because there aren't many trees and from what I can gather fires like getting into trees.

Emily, thanks so much for your advice about my parents, but I don't think it's much use. I mean, from my experience, they *have* stayed together 'because of the children', and it's done no good at all. Thank you very much for praying about them, but would God really be interested in those two? I'm sure he has better things to worry about, like starving Africans and even bushfires. Weren't you lucky you had so many relatives there to help you!

You might hate to come from a broken home, but that's only because your home sounds happy, and your pink bedroom is probably an idyllic haven. At the moment my mother is sharing my room. She sleeps on a beanbag. Heaven knows why (why she's sharing my room, I mean. She sleeps on the beanbag because she enjoys discomfort). And she snores, and talks in her sleep.

I had a talk to Dad, as I told you I would. He said that 'people have to work at relationships' and that Mum was 'going through a period of change'. It is very difficult to get any sense from my father, because he talks like a public servant. Everything he says is sort of pre-packaged, if you know what I mean. Like our food now.

Only eleven days to go before I'm fifteen. Yes, I promise to send a photo of us all soon, and the flat.

So pleased things are still on, as you put it, with Kevin. You probably need a boyfriend in the country, particularly with the bushfires and everything.

Lots of love,

Maria

Dear Emily,

I hope you don't think I mentioned my birthday in my last letter just to get a present. It just slipped out. After I posted the letter I realised I'd mentioned the date.

Hope you haven't had any more fires.

Love,

Maria

Dear Emily,

Well, my birthday was a wash-out. Would you believe, the only person who remembered was G. F. Smales? And guess what the creep gave me? A second-hand book, *How To Improve Your Mind*. What a nerve. He's definitely getting rat poison for his.

Of course Mum and Dad *did* remember when they saw his present. Mum cried and said she felt terrible for forgetting her daughter's birthday but she had so much on her mind. Dad gave me twenty dollars and said 'spend it wisely'.

Mum's promised to take me to the market to buy some white jeans and a striped blouse. We'll probably go on Sunday. Last night she bought four take-away pizzas for my birthday tea and she drank glasses and glasses of moselle and started to cry again about what a terrible mother she is for forgetting her daughter's birthday.

Now that I think of it, she isn't much of a mother, to tell the truth. I am getting pimples again, and I know it's because of the rotten food she's getting these days. Maybe she'll get her health food kick back again soon. She never stays on anything for long.

Anyway, just thought I'd let you know about how my birthday went.

Please write soon.

Your friend forever,
Maria

Dear Emily,

Oh, thank you so much for my present! It arrived this morning, and here I was thinking you'd forgotten my birthday too! It is wonderful to have a real friend like you, Emily.

The necklace is just beautiful. I've never had a necklace before. I didn't know they had such lovely things in country towns. You are just so kind.

I am sorry to have upset your parents by saying what I did about the burnt cows. Honest, I didn't mean any harm. I mean, it was awful that they were burnt, and it just struck me at the time that it would be a pity to waste all that meat, and they were sort of barbecued already. Please tell them I am very sorry, and I was not trying to be smart, as your father suggested.

Actually I am surprised they took it so personally. I mean, you eat steak all the time in the country, don't you?

What *did* you do with all that free meat, anyway? There must be so many poor people in the country who would have loved even one chop.

Yes, my mother still has her beanbag in my room. We do have a sofa in the lounge room, but its springs stick into you if you lie on it. It's okay to sit on watching telly if you watch where you sit.

The other night I talked to Mum for an hour or so about her and Dad splitting up, and she didn't see my point of view at all. She said, 'These things will all be worked through, Maria, it just takes time.' No idea what she meant. Frankly, I don't think *she* does, either. She's got that from some group meeting, that's for sure.

School starts in nine days. I'm quite pleased, because the holidays have been boring. Yes, I still swim in the pool, and tell your father that I am *not* dreaming about having a pool on top of our flats. I get the impression he doesn't altogether like me, what with the cow comments and saying I dream things up. Still, being a farmer, he probably isn't used to anything out of the ordinary.

Thanks again *so very much* for my wonderful necklace. I'll wear it under my blouse to school.

Your friend forever,

Maria

P.S. Bet you're sick of riding horses every day!

Dear Emily,

I think it was a waste to bury the cows, but it's none of my business.

Your class teacher sounds terrific. Fancy coming outside and eating his lunch with you all! The staffroom at our school is like a bank vault. You have to knock so many times for certain teachers, and they *hate* seeing you at lunch time. They come out with a cup of coffee and half eaten roll and *stare* at you and say 'Well?' The idea of any of my teachers eating lunch with me is impossible.

Maybe country teachers are more childish and enjoy talking to students, I don't know. Now that I'm fifteen, there are so many things I don't know, Emily. When I was thirteen I thought I knew just about everything.

The Start of Year Bush Dance sounds interesting. Thanks for sending that little piece of material from your dress — it's so pretty — pink again! I think you're very clever making your dress yourself. I suppose you save lots of money that way. Do all people in the country make their own clothes? Oh, in the rush of getting everything ready for school I forgot the photos. Sorry. Next letter, promise.

I have some plans to make myself more interesting. I mean, it's not that I'm not, I just feel I've done nothing with my holidays except try to talk my parents into splitting up, and that's been a failure. Mum's back sleeping in their bedroom now, so my efforts at splitting up the Smales household were a complete flop.

Here are my plans:

1. Read a book a week
2. Speak to a stranger who looks lonely every week
3. Start a diary about my life
4. Learn to say hello in ten languages
5. Learn all I can about Death Duties
6. Get cookery books out of the library and learn to cook exotic things.

What do you think, Emily?

I mean, *one* of my family has to be remembered for something. In years to come, people will say, 'I knew Maria Smales. She was a fascinating girl.' Hey, if you keep all my letters, maybe one day you could get them published!

Lots of love,
your fascinating, interesting friend,

Maria

Dear Emily,

Here at last are some photos. Our flat is the one I've put an X on. You can't see the pool because it's on the roof. The one of me was taken by G. F. Smales, which is why I'm not smiling. I didn't take one of him because I thought it would break the camera.

Mum and Dad didn't want to have their photos taken, and I see their point. As I mentioned, Mum without makeup and proper clothes is not up to much, and taking a photo of Dad is a bit pointless when you come to think about it. It would just depress you.

I was interested to hear what you thought of my plan to make myself more interesting. You could be right about the plan of speaking to strangers. The one I spoke to last week told me to go away (well, that's what he meant, but he put it pretty nastily) and to mind my own business. I felt sorry for him because he was sitting on the footpath drinking something out of a bottle in a brown paper bag and he looked so miserable. But I suppose I shouldn't have tried to cheer him up.

I can say hello in seven languages now — I asked kids at school (in the city we have multi-cultural schools, which means students come from all sorts of interesting places). It must be dull at the country school to have only Australians there. I can say hello in Italian, Greek, Vietnamese, Turkish, Maltese, Lebanese and English. How about that? The problem is when I say hello to people in their own language they answer in English. Anyway, I'm sure they think I'm clever for bothering.

I haven't learnt anything yet about Death Duties and tell your father I don't agree it's a morbid subject. I saw something on telly about them, and I really believe the government should take rich people's money when they die and help poor people with it. Your father sounds uninformed if he thinks there shouldn't be any. He probably worries about milking the cows too much and doesn't read or watch telly.

Actually, Emily, maybe you'd better not show my letters to him, I don't think he is sophisticated enough to appreciate letters from the city.

I am humbled that you have kept all my letters. Yes, I have started my diary. It is, of course, for future publication, so unfortunately it can't be too personal. I'll send you an exotic recipe for lamb soon.

> Lots of love,
> your humbled and exotic friend,
> Maria

Dear Emily,

I am so pleased you like the photo. Yes, I know I look sad, but I explained why in my letter so you can go back and look up why I wasn't smiling. You mustn't have read my letter properly.

Tell your father that the flats might look cramped and ugly but that is an outside photo. Inside they are quite luxurious. Actually I think I explained about that some letters ago — flats that look beautiful from the outside attract burglars. Your father certainly hasn't been around much. I bet he is a country innocent.

I have *definitely* stopped talking to strangers. The last one I tried asked if I was on drugs or something. As if I'd be that stupid. All I did was tell her what a wonderful day it was to be alive in.

Your school sounds more idyllic every time you mention it. It must be great having lunch with teachers under spreading trees. What about ants?

Emily, please thank your mother very much for the invitation to come and stay with you at Easter. It is very kind of her, but you see, I can't, because we are going to Sydney for Easter. I would have loved to, really I would.

You see, the train fare to see you would be heaps,

and Dad gets a free rail pass to Sydney being in the railways and everything.

I am sure we'll meet one day, I just know it!

You are asking again about G. F. Smales! Look, this is the sort of creep he is. He goes out at night and takes garden gnomes from people's front yards. I don't suppose you have them in the country, but some people have them here. They are concrete monsters, with little red caps.

Then he puts them in his room, and after a few days he returns them to the gardens he nicked them from. He puts a note with them which tells their owners they had a nice holiday.

He thinks that is smart. So, no more questions about him, please! As you can see from that, he is very unbalanced.

I've got to go to the library now to get some exotic recipes — will send exotic lamb recipe soon.

Love,
and have a wonderful Easter,
Maria

Dear Emily,

Received your letter this morning. Fancy you going to Sydney at Easter! When was that decided? Oh, I'm so disappointed, because Dad has cancelled our Sydney trip! What a pity, when you would have been there.

I didn't realise you meant I could come to see you and go with you to Sydney. It would be wonderful to see the Royal Easter Show, and to watch you and your horse.

Your parents are very kind to offer to take me with them to Sydney, Emily. Unfortunately we are going to Perth for Easter and I can't make it. Dad gets a free air ticket because he's a public servant. But I wish you luck with your horse. Will you be sleeping with it again?

You must be very happy that Kevin is coming with you to Sydney too. Just think, if things had worked out, I could have met him too. Next time!
Better rush and work out what to take to Perth.

Have a great Easter,
love,
Maria

P.S. No, I haven't tried praying again. Maybe I will soon.

Dear Emily,

Thanks so much for your postcard from Sydney, and your letter. The Opera House looks wonderful. You must have been thrilled to see it, as you wouldn't see anything like that in the country.

I'm sorry I didn't send a postcard from Perth. I forgot to buy stamps. Yes, we had a cosmic time. (Look up cosmic, it's the newest word in the city.)

Congratulations on winning another ribbon for your horse. Do you hang them round his neck?

No, I haven't been to The Rocks. Or maybe I have when I was small, because we used to go just *everywhere*, but I can't remember. Do people fish off them or something? What's so interesting about seeing rocks, anyway? Surely you have lots of rocks on your farm.

Here is the lamb recipe. I will pray that it turns out for you.

Exotic Lamb a la Maria

Buy four lamb chops (you probably have a few lambs around so you can get free ones). Marinade (that means soak) them in one tablespoon honey, one tablespoon soy sauce (if you can't get that in the country, just use tomato sauce), pepper and salt, one teaspoon ginger and two tablespoons oil. Leave them for two hours, then grill them. The recipe from the library book said to add one tablespoon of sherry to the marinade if desired. I'm not desired but I suppose Kevin desires you so you might as well add it.

They taste really cosmic, and Mum even had one. She's back into meat now.

I have discovered, by reading a lot, that a certain kind of person approves of death duties, and another kind of person is against them. Rich people are against them, and poor people are for them. It's very simple, really. I suppose how much money you have more or less decides how you think about things.

Would you describe yourself as political? I'm beginning to be. Maybe politics don't matter in the country, because there aren't many people to control, but I think they are important in the life of an urban person (urban means city).

Must do some more political reading. Good luck with the lamb chops!

Your friend forever,

Maria

Dear Emily,

I'm so glad the chops were successful!

Wonderful news. G. F. Smales has migrated north! He says he can't stand being cooped up here (not that he's ever home, and anyway, our flat is luxurious, as I've mentioned). Mum was upset and Dad seemed really pleased. He says he'll look for work, but it would be just like his sleazy mind to look for the nearest dole office instead.

Maybe a shark will get him. I'll pray tonight!

He was skipping school anyway, so he had no future here really. He is not a welcome addition to the human race. But I've heard people are unusual up north, so maybe he'll fit in and not be noticed. I hope never to see him again. We are not a close family.

At the moment Mum is into something you'll never have heard of (nor had I) called primal therapy.

It's sheer madness. I asked her about it all, and it's the sort of ridiculous thing that would appeal to someone with a brain the size of a pea (e.g. my mother).

A group of idiots sit about and imagine they are being *born again* and they curl up like a baby in the womb (I suppose you know the facts of life, Emily, even though you live in the country). Some of them even cry, like a baby.

There's a bit more to it but I won't bore you with details. Enough to say that my mother has gone off her tiny brain

She says it gives her strength to 'cope with herself'. I have given up.

The only positive thing to come out of it is she's so busy 'coping with herself' she hasn't time to cope with anything else, so I get to do the cooking. When she was a health food freak she wouldn't let me cook anything but now that she's into convenience cooking and meat again she doesn't care.

No, I didn't think from your letters that you were political. In fact, anything but, because all you write about is Kevin, dances, school, horses and clothes. You haven't exactly got a lot of interesting interests, have you, Emily?

But I don't mind. I really understand what it must be like living with horses and cows and things and having such small experiences. I'm sure it is just so idyllic and rustic (look it up).

No, I still haven't got a boyfriend, but, as I've mentioned before, I don't need one. My political interests take up so much time these days. I watch three news programmes every night now that G. F. Smales is gone (he was a cretin and never watched the news, like you).

Must go. Am working on a great sausage and bean casserole. If it works, will send the recipe.

Your friend forever, politically,

Maria

Dear Emily,

Look, Emily, no hard feelings, but I really think you shouldn't show my letters to your parents if they continue to make awful comments about them.

I think it is rude of them to say country kids know more about the facts of life than city kids because they see it happening. I just don't believe your parents would do things like that in front of you.

That is terrible. My parents, I'm sure, don't do those things any more, because they are in their late thirties, but, if they did, they certainly wouldn't let anyone see them. The whole idea is mind-boggling. I mean, it must put you off getting married!

And they are not at all fair saying I'm nasty to wish that a shark gets my brother. They simply do not know how horrendous G. F. Smales is, so they needn't comment.

And I was *not* being unkind when I said you had no interesting interests. You haven't! So what? You are my dearest friend and I treasure our friendship. Haven't they heard that opposites attract?

I really think it is too much to devote one whole letter to criticising my letter. You should be grateful someone writes to you at all in such a remote place.

I look forward to hearing from you and *not* about what your parents have to say about my letters!

Yours sincerely,
with deeply hurt feelings,
Maria

Dear Emily,

Although I have not heard from you since last I wrote, I have remembered your birthday. Not that you deserve it, at the moment.

Here is a diary for you. I chose it because of the pink plastic cover. Remember I wrote and said I was going to start a diary about my life? Well, I have, and I thought you might like to start one too, even though you'll probably write about Kevin, clothes, dances, school and horses. But I suppose if that's all there is to your life, that's all you can write about! C'est la vie! (That's French for 'That's life'.)

I hope you like the card, too, and the pink rabbits on the front of it. I thought it was appropriate for a country girl who likes pink.

I look forward to hearing from you.

Yours sincerely,
Maria

Dear Emily,

Thank you for your letter.

I am glad you liked your diary, and I hope you enjoy writing in it.

Emily, I must apologise to you. When your parents said country kids know more about the facts of life because they see it happening, I didn't realise they meant cows and bulls and dogs. How would I know that, being an urban person? I really feel very stupid about thinking it was your parents, not your animals. I have hardly ever had to apologise about anything in my life, and this is very hard for me to do, but on this occasion I think I should. Don't you? I don't agree with them that horses-Kevin-school-dances-clothes are healthier interests for girls of our age than saying unkind things about family members. It's all very well for you, your family seem simple, but, as I've explained hundreds of times, mine leave a lot to be desired.

I still think, if our correspondence is to continue, you should not show them my letters. They seem to take everything I say the wrong way.

Will you accept my apology, Emily?

Your humbled friend,

Maria

71

Dear Emily,

Thank you for accepting my apology. I am humbled.

But, my dear friend, you are still reading things into my letters which were not meant!

I did not mean your family was simple minded! I meant they seem to live a simple, uncomplicated life, and you don't have the horrendous urban problems I have, what with Mum joining primal therapy groups and changing her eating habits every week, and Dad leading a public service life style. I will be very careful what I write to you in future, because you obviously (or your parents, or all of you) have a problem understanding what I mean.

I didn't respond to the comment your father made ages ago about it not being true that public servants get free plane fares, because I knew he simply didn't know what he was talking about. But, seeing you've mentioned he said it again, tell him from me that he is wrong. He's never been a public servant, so how would he know? And anyway, what does he mean it's his taxes that pay for public servants? How does he know whose taxes they are? I think he should stick to milking cows and not get involved in political arguments.

School is terrible. The papers have been having

articles about Teacher Burn Out, which means that teachers get really sick and tired of their job because it's so demanding, so a few of my teachers decided they had it. We have some emergency teachers who don't know what work we've been doing and don't know the kids so nothing much in the way of education is happening. I don't think country teachers would get Teacher Burn Out, unless they read about it in the papers. Do you get papers in the country?

I'm sorry you and Kevin have split up. You seem upset about it, Emily. But surely you'd like a change? I'd get terribly bored with the same boyfriend for over a year, I'm sure.

Yes, we have heard from G. F. Smales. He sent Mum and Dad a postcard with a girl in a bikini on it and he is, as I predicted, *on the dole*. I told you he was a creep.

I'd better go. With all this Teacher Burn Out I have to read a lot to keep educated!

Your friend forever,

Maria

Dear Emily,

Well, it was great to get such a happy letter from you, with no complaints about my letters for a change!

Maybe you've seen the light and have stopped showing my letters to your parents. I hope so.

I am pleased because you're so pleased that you and Kevin have made it up. Made what up? You country people certainly have some strange expressions.

No, I don't agree with you that praying to God helped about you and Kevin. I mean, with all the global (that means worldwide) problems he has to solve, I don't really think he can be bothered with a lovers' quarrel, do you, if you think about it?

But, on the other hand, I *did* try praying that G. F. Smales would go north, and he did. I suppose I have to keep an open mind about God.

I didn't realise you got all the city papers in the country. There's no excuse for your father's lack of knowledge about politics, then.

Your new dress for the school dance sounds just divine. Idyllically divine. Pink check with white lace collar and cuffs. Wow. Yes, I would love a photo of you and Kevin in your dance clothes. I know I haven't sent any more photos, but I will soon.

The sausage and bean casserole was terrific. It's easy. Just heat a bit of oil in a saucepan and put in two sliced onions and two sliced tomatoes. Cook them for a while, until they are soft, then take them out and cook some sausages (two each) in oil. Then add the onions and tomatoes, some salt and pepper, and a can of red kidney beans and some oregano.

Maybe you can't get red kidney beans in the country, so baked beans will do. And I suppose you've never heard of oregano. It's a herb and you get it in packets at supermarkets. I suppose you could use parsley in the country.

Let me know how it goes. My mother is now on a high fibre diet and eats bran for all her meals. Her brain has completely flipped. Dad and I ate all the sausages and beans.

Have a great time at the dance. I'd have thought you'd be sick of school dances and pink clothes by now. Yes, I'm still reading one book a week. Can't you tell how it's improved my writing?

Must go to the library.

Lots of love,

Maria

Dear Emily,

You asked if we had heard again from G. F. Smales. Yes. Unfortunately. He is now *off the dole* and selling surfboards in a surfie shop. Would you believe it?

Yes, he likes it up north. From what I've read about people up there he probably would. They don't have any Death Duties and there is lots of sun so there are probably hundreds of dropouts like G. F. there. At least the sun might clear up his ugly pimples. I can't see why you ever ask about him. When I first wrote to you I said he was better ignored and I have had no reason to change my mind on that.

Take my advice and stick to simple country boys. I bet no one has pimples in the country because of all that fresh air.

I'm still reading a lot to keep educated. You don't mention that you read much, and from your letters I guess you mustn't. Still, it takes all sorts to make this world, I always say, don't you?

Emily, you would never want to hear from G. F. Smales or write to him. If he sends you a postcard (he might, remember when he read your letters and wanted to write?) *ignore* it.

Feed it to your chooks. Now that he's working

he'll think he's big time and will try to impress anyone (even you) with his bad taste postcards.

I'd better get back to reading *The Getting of Wisdom*. You should try reading it — it's about a country girl like you who comes to the city and of course can't cope with it all. You will probably find it a bit difficult after your teenage magazines, but it will be an education for you.

Love, forever,

Maria

Dear Emily,

Thank you for the lovely photo of you and Kevin. You must have dozens of you both by now.

I love your hair tied up like that with the flowers in it. Don't they wilt and die while you're dancing?

Fancy your mother growing oregano. And here was I thinking you'd never heard of it! And your local grocer has tins of red kidney beans! The country is certainly improving, isn't it? I am glad you all enjoyed the sausage and bean casserole, and I'll try your suggestion about adding some paprika. I didn't realise you'd know anything about herbs and spices, but, as I've said before, I know there's a lot I have to learn.

I am rather upset at what your father said about me. Do you really mean that if I make another comment about him you won't be allowed to write to me any more? That's terrible, Emily! I so depend on your letters. He is trying to curb your creativity (how's that for an expression!). I mean, you must so look forward to hearing all the urban news from me. But I take the hint. From here on I won't mention the idiot.

No, Mum hasn't changed her diet again yet. I think she will soon, because the last packet of bran she opened had weevils or something in it, and that's put her off a bit, although I pointed out they were probably full of protein and people in Ethiopia would give anything for weevily bran. But, as usual, she didn't see the point.

I'm really bugged about what your father said. My parents never mention you — mind you, I've never shown them your letters, I consider them my private property. I wish you'd shown the same *restraint*. Fancy him going on about what I said about stuffing Blackie and the facts of life and all that. That was *years* ago! Show some moral fibre (which Dad says Mum should do instead of eating it) and keep my letters to yourself.

I'm too angry to write any more. I hope you are upset because you have caused this anger by showing *private* correspondence to your dumb and overbearing father. Your mother is probably quite nice, and I'm sure you are, too.

Your friend,
in anger,
Maria Smales
P.S. I bet he doesn't know what Bastille Day is!!!

Dear Emily,

I am not really surprised that I haven't heard from you, given that you live in a prison and do whatever your father tells you to. I mean, urban fathers don't tell you to do anything except go to school and go to the milk bar for the papers.

And here I was being envious of your idyllic and rustic parents!

Anyway, I'll tell you *my* news. I won an essay competition at school (all this reading and writing to you and keeping my diary has really helped my English expression) and guess what? I won *fifty dollars!*

I have never had more than twenty dollars (Dad's birthday present last year) in my life. This is wonderful, I just *had* to tell you, as you're my closest friend, in spite of your parentage.

I'm going to get two goldfish and a fish bowl, a new T shirt, some sneakers, and twelve sticks of liquorice. I can't believe it. I haven't told Mum, because she'd want a cut, and she decided to give up her Avon job as a cosmetic executive so she shouldn't complain about being poor. (We aren't poor, of course, it's just that Mum gets things out of perspective.)

I hope you like this pink lacy hanky — I saw it

and thought of you, and, seeing that I'm divinely rich at the moment, I thought a kind gift would be appropriate.

The fifty dollars has made my anger go away a bit.

Lots of love,

Maria

P.S. Hope you like the hanky!

Dear Emily,

Have you received the hanky? Does Kevin like it? Is it the right shade of pink? Does it match your dresses?

How are your parents and your cows? And horses?

How is school? And Kevin? When is your next school dance?

I bought the goldfish and have called them Emily and Kevin. I thought that would be a kind thing to do. Don't you agree?

They are very beautiful and swim around together all the time, a bit like you and Kevin, I'm sure.

Until I hear from you,
your friend forever,

Maria

Dear Emily,

It is over a month since I have heard from you. Surely you can write to me and not tell your father? Write at school instead of having your idyllic lunches with teachers under the trees, and post it on the way home.

You really can't let your life be ruled by your father, Emily, particularly as he's a farmer. Farmers might be the salt of the earth and all that, but they don't know much about human relationships, only animal relationships. Well, maybe some do, but I don't think your father is one of them.

Anyway, it's only polite to write and thank me for that pink hanky!

Kevin and Emily are just fine. They are great company now that I don't have your letters to look forward to. Goldfish aren't exactly the most exciting pets to have, but you know where they are, they don't smell, and it's relaxing to just watch them chase one another all over the bowl. Emily is bigger than Kevin, she eats more.

School isn't too bad at the moment. We have an emergency Maths teacher (our regular one has the famous and catching Teacher Burn Out) who is really funny. He talks to us about his girlfriend and his cat and how he gets drunk and stoned every night. I've never met anyone like him. He is really very educational and has opened my eyes to another side of urban life.

I can use a calculator anyway so Maths isn't worth bothering about. I tell you, I'm learning about real life, not equations!

How is your horse? Here are two envelopes of sugar (can't fit more in the envelope) I nicked from a coffee bar for him. I read in one of my books that horses like sugar.

I have been praying that you will write to me. Let's hope God is plugged in up there and gets the message.

Mum is now on a dairy product free diet, which, as I told her, doesn't help the dairy farmers (like your father). So, you see, I'm willing to forgive his meddling in our relationship. If you still all go to church, he should forgive me too (not that there's anything to forgive!) because Christians are into this forgiving business.

Not much more news.

Until I hear from you,
yours prayerfully,

Maria

84

Dearest Emily,

Thank you so much for your letter! Maybe you're right about God!

But I am sorry you returned the envelopes of sugar. What do you mean, you can't accept stolen goods? Look, Emily, I don't take sugar in coffee, and at the local coffee bar they always put two envelopes of suger on the saucer. I usually leave them, but I thought your horse might appreciate them. That's *not* stealing. I mean, I paid for the coffee, and that includes the sugar. I bet your father put you up to that, you're far too nice to send those back of your own free will.

I am rather upset by that. I enclose them again with this letter and please think through carefully what I've just written to you on this subject. Fancy depriving a dumb animal because of your father!

I don't like your suggestion that I should talk to the Principal about the emergency Maths teacher. That's silly. We are learning so much about real life, you've no idea — well, his version of real life. Just because he gets drunk and stoned doesn't mean *we* are going to — in fact, he makes it all sound pretty messy! Some people can run their lives and some can't. I can, he can't, it's all very clear. But we give him lots of advice. Terry Goma, who sits next to me, worked out what percentage of his salary went on booze and dope, and I tell you, he really thought about that one! Said he had to cut down. Now, if that isn't practical Maths, what is?

Also kids have been bringing him articles about alcohol and drug abuse. Emily, we can all help one another in this world, even at school! You must have a very old-fashioned view of life if you think teachers help students, and that's it. It *can* work the other way, you know. We are helping *him*. I bet going to the Principal was your father's idea.

Your letter was pretty short. I'm pleased you liked the hanky and it was the right shade of pink. I can't quite understand your father thinking I'm a bad influence on you, because we've never met, and you don't seem to learn anything at all from my views on things, you're still the simple country girl I started writing to eighteen months ago. He is an insular person (look that up).

I must go to the library now. I'm collecting statistics on alcoholism and its effects on the brain for our emergency teacher before he becomes an emergency case.

Lots of love,
your non-influential friend,
Maria

Dear Emily,

So you did give the sugar to your horse, good on you! Do you want more?

I am not surprised to hear that it was your father's idea to go to the Principal, and no, I won't tell you the name of the teacher, because you never know what your father would do.

He is a very nice person (the teacher, not you know who) and we are really helping him to sort out his life. He's even begun to teach us a sort of computer Maths, which is very interesting. A few of us have coffee with him after school, which stops him going to the pub (he says) and I really feel we are doing a useful service to a human being in need.

Good luck with your horse at the show this year. It's a pity your father won't let you meet me, because we aren't going on holidays this time. Dad says they have stopped the free fares for public servants, and anyway, Mum isn't speaking to him at the moment, so a holiday would be pretty silent, seeing Dad hardly ever speaks to either of us at the best of times. Mum says she might go and see G. F. Smales up north, but I have warned her against that!

G. F. Smales is still selling surfboards, seeing you asked. I can see you take no notice of my advice at all. He has learnt to ride surfboards, and I pray nightly (see, I take your advice, I now pray) that he'll fall off and be carried out the sea. So far God has not answered my prayers.

Thank you for including me in your prayers, Emily, but to be honest I can't quite see why. My life and my personality have developed so much over the last year, can't you tell from my letters?

The goldfish are fine — well, as far as one can ever tell about goldfish.

We are taking our teacher to the zoo over the holidays. Would you believe, he's never been there?

I am surprised your father knew all about Bastille Day! I didn't think he was educated. In fact I thought his interests were milking cows and God and reading my letters. Just shows how wrong I can be!

Your new dress for the Show Ball sounds divine. I suppose Kevin will be going with you. I'll tell my goldfish.

Take care of yourself, Emily, and tell your father to mind his own business. I will not have him making comments about my teacher when he doesn't even know him. He is certainly the best teacher I've ever had, and a very nice, if confused, person. He wouldn't dream of telling your father how to run his life, even if he had the misfortune to know him.

Your friend forever,
Marca

Dear Emily,

I can't believe your last letter.

You can't possibly mean that you will never write to me again because of the things I've said about your father. What about him? He started it all, making comments about my letters. I mean I don't even *know* him, and he says I'm a bad influence on you, and I have an 'unhealthy relationship' with my teacher! You told me you have lunch with your teachers, all I've done is have coffee (enclosed are four sugar envelopes for your horse) with mine, and anyway there's four of us who go and have coffee with him, not just me. I've never even been alone with him!

That's what comes from living in the country, I always knew it. Even if your father has been to University, he certainly hasn't had many experiences.

I feel very sad and angry about all this, because I have tried so hard to expand your view of the world, and regard you as my closest friend. I have all your photos up in my bedroom, and all your bookmarks.

I even named my fish after you and Kevin! Who else would do that? Incidentally, Kevin died yesterday. I flushed him down the toilet but I'll get another one and Emily won't know the difference.

I'd have buried him but we have no ground at these flats, and anyway flushing's better for a fish, don't you think?

I am sure you *will* write to me again. You couldn't just stop a friendship like that.

My mother is still into her primal therapy experiences. Maybe if your father had had a few of those he'd be more understanding of other people (not that it's helped Mum much, I must say).

I look forward to hearing from you, Emily. I do not believe you will be dictated to by your father.

I am a healthy, vital urban female and wish to continue sharing my thoughts with my dear country penfriend.

Yours ever,
Marca

Dear Emily,

In vain I have waited for a letter.

Here are four more sugar envelopes.

Your friend forever,

Maria

Dear Emily,

I have bought another fish and have called it Black-ie, after your dead dog. I thought you would appreciate that.

I hope you won ribbons for your horse again at the show, and that you and Kevin enjoyed the Show Ball. I looked in the papers to see if there were any pictures of you at the Show — they often have pictures of people with horses around Show time. I suppose country papers have those all year round.

It is nearly three weeks since you wrote and said you wouldn't be writing again. That's a long time to wait for a letter!

Our emergency teacher has gone to another school for a week. We all hope the kids there will take care of him and try to help him as much as we have.

I have decided to dedicate my life to people who need help. Maybe I'll try to get involved in Community Aid Abroad because then I could help people and see the world at the same time. Mum says I have to be a lot older so maybe I'll join some voluntary organisation here first. It's not that I'm wonderfully kind or anything, I just get such a buzz out of helping people. My father says it's selfish. That seems a pretty odd thing to say, but then, as you know, fathers can say some pretty odd things at times!

How is your father? Still milking and going to church and stopping you from writing to your best friend? Tell him I forgive him but can't understand why he makes you suffer.

Please write soon.

Yours forever,

Maria

Dear Emily,

There has been a postal strike here for two days and if you have written your letter will be held up, so I thought I'd write again so you wouldn't feel ignored.

The good news is our teacher is back again and we'll have him for Maths until the end of the year! He said he's stopped doing all the silly things he was doing because we helped him 'find himself'! And here was I thinking only my mother did things like that. She's been looking for herself for some time now, but I don't think she's been too successful.

Tell your father I've started some voluntary work, I'm sure he'd approve. I read books to old people with poor eyesight. It's fun, you get to go to their flats, and they give you tea and biscuits, and you read them romance stories.

The stories are a bit silly (though you might like them as you have a boyfriend and like all that stuff) but it is broadening my mind in all directions.

They are all about people blushing and breathing deeply and straining other people to their bosoms. But the old ladies really love them.

Tell your father they are very *proper* (the stories, and probably the old ladies too) and everyone gets married and lives happily ever after. They are fiction, of course, and not about life as we know it at all.

How is Kevin? Have you made any pink dresses lately? Do you use the hanky I gave you?

Please answer these questions when you write.

Love,

Maria

Dear Emily,

Just to let you know the postal strike is over.

I really miss getting your letters. I suppose I'll have to get another country penfriend if you don't write to me soon. That would be a pity, because it took me so long to get used to your life style of dresses and dances and horses and Kevin, I don't know if I could start all that again.

So *please* write soon.

Your urban penfriend,

Maria

Dear Emily,

I have decided to give you until Melbourne Cup Day to answer my letters.

For the life of me I can't understand why you don't!

The goldfish and my teacher are fine. I told my teacher all about you and your idiot father and he said I shouldn't worry so much about it and you probably just outgrew me.

I think that's a *strange* comment. If anything, it's the other way round! I mean, you can see from my letters how I've developed over the time we've been writing but you have always been a sweet, simple country girl.

So, if I don't hear by Melbourne Cup Day, this is goodbye.

Your sad friend,

Maria

Dear Emily,

You will not hear from me again.

One day I hope you will realise how unhappy you have made me. Just when I have decided to dedicate my life to helping people, too!

I bet you'll end up married to Kevin and milking cows together and having lots of little daughters, and you'll dress them in pink, and that's just what you deserve for breaking off our relationship.

I just hope all country people aren't like you. If they are, what hope have we for the future?

I am advertising for a new country penfriend and I hope she will be tolerant and interesting and want to learn about life.

I hope you have kept my letters to read to your grandchildren so they can learn a little about the world.

From

Maria Smales

P.S. The funny thing is, I really liked you.

About the author

Maureen Stewart was involved in teaching and education for over twenty years, both in Australia and overseas. She has had over forty books published, as well as articles and short stories. For the last two years she has been writing full time, and claims this has been the happiest time of her life.

Apart from writing, she likes friends, hot curries and hot beaches. She dislikes unkindness and committees.

Maureen lives with her husband, a dog and a retarded cat in Richmond, Victoria. She has one grown-up son, Cameron.

ORANGE WENDY
Maureen Stewart

When you're fifteen and fat, there seems little hope of ever having a boyfriend. At least, so Wendy thought, till a hot Brisbane summer and a lucky accident changed her mind.

For days afterwards her life was turned upside down, and things happened to her that she had never dreamed were possible.

Not all of what happened was fun. Some of it was tragedy, and she learned a hard lesson. But it was all part of Wendy's orange summer, and she tells her funny and moving story as honestly as she can.

HATING ALISON ASHLEY
Robin Klein

Life was difficult at Barringa East Primary
where the teachers tended to have nervous
problems and everyone called you 'Yuk'.

However, Erica Yurken knew she was destined
for a glittering career on the stage. She had
never had any doubts about her own genius.
She felt superior to everyone in Barringa East,
even the School Principal and the visiting
District Inspector.

That is, until Alison Ashley started at Barringa
East Primary . . .

Alison Ashley excelled at everything. She was
beautiful, rich, clever and as well-behaved as a
nativity angel. She also lived outside Barringa
East – on exclusive Hedge End Road.

But Erica was determined to show up Alison
Ashley – and the annual school camp would be
the ideal place!

TAYLOR'S TROUBLES
Lowell Tarling

'I want to go to the toilet already. I have only just arrived in high school and I want to go. Primary school kids can't wait, but when you get into high school you've got to learn these things ...'

So begins Tommy Taylor's first day at high school. Straight from primary school, where he was labelled troublesome, Tommy Taylor starts high school with the best of intentions. But when he is initiated by the Hood, caned by Bull McTodd and rejected by Carol, he quickly decides there are far more exciting challenges – such as being in a rock group and learning the Johnny Robbo walk ...

THREE WAY STREET
Bron Nicholls

Aggie lives with her mum, sister and brothers
in an inner-city suburb. The back yards are
small and made of concrete, but the front doors
open onto the street, where things happen. The
street dogs hang out here too, learning to look
after themselves, just like the kids.

It all began with the new pup that mum
grudgingly let them keep (to save its neck) and
then the artist bloke moved in across the
street . . .

Three Way Street tells of one important year in
Aggie's life, and of her efforts to make sense
out of growing up.

THE DINGBAT SPIES
Joan Flanagan

When 'Tangletoes' Latimer announces that the
family are moving house, his wife escapes
hastily to Budapest, the housekeeper resigns,
and the pet budgie flies away. So the moving is
left to his long-suffering children and the
extraordinarily untalented rock group, The
Fallen Angels, which Latimer manages.

But the new house is no ordinary house – the
toaster talks, there are secret passages,
mysterious telephones in strange places, and
computers that issue the oddest information.
Not to mention the strange uniformed
neighbours who move into their house in the
depths of night . . .

CLOSER TO THE STARS
Max Fatchen

1941 ... and at the airforce base near Paul's
farm, pilots are being trained for the war.
Meanwhile they play games with their planes –
barnstorming haystacks and frightening the
townfolk – and then one of them becomes
involved with Paul's sister, Nancy.

But when Nancy discovers she is pregnant, it is
Paul who must help her confront the uncertain
future, the hostile attitudes of small-town
gossips ... and the ultimate shattering blow.

HEARD ABOUT THE PUFFIN CLUB?

... it's a way of finding out more about Puffin books
and authors, of winning prizes (in competitions),
sharing jokes, a secret code, and perhaps
seeing your name in print! When you join you get a copy
of our magazine, *Puffinalia*, sent to you
four times a year, a badge and a membership book.
For details of subscription and an application form, send
a stamped addressed envelope to:

*The Australian Puffin Club
Penguin Books Australia Limited
P.O. Box 257
Ringwood
Victoria 3134*

and if you live in the UK, for a copy of *Puffin Post*
please write to:

*The Puffin Club Dept A
Penguin Books Limited
Bath Road
Harmondsworth
Middlesex UB7 ODA2*